T5-AGP-627

Free the Worms!

by Nancy Krulik • illustrated by John & Wendy

Grosset & Dunlap

For Sarah and Emily—N.K.
For Judy—friend of the little guy!—J&W

GROSSET & DUNLAP
Published by the Penguin Group
Penguin Group (USA) Inc., 375 Hudson Street, New York, New York 10014, USA
Penguin Group (Canada), 90 Eglinton Avenue East, Suite 700, Toronto,
Ontario M4P 2Y3, Canada
(a division of Pearson Penguin Canada Inc.)
Penguin Books Ltd., 80 Strand, London WC2R 0RL, England
Penguin Group Ireland, 25 St. Stephen's Green, Dublin 2, Ireland
(a division of Penguin Books Ltd.)
Penguin Group (Australia), 250 Camberwell Road, Camberwell,
Victoria 3124, Australia
(a division of Pearson Australia Group Pty. Ltd.)
Penguin Books India Pvt. Ltd., 11 Community Centre, Panchsheel Park,
New Delhi—110 017, India
Penguin Group (NZ), 67 Apollo Drive, Rosedale, North Shore 0632, New Zealand
(a division of Pearson New Zealand Ltd.)
Penguin Books (South Africa) (Pty.) Ltd., 24 Sturdee Avenue,
Rosebank, Johannesburg 2196, South Africa

Penguin Books Ltd., Registered Offices: 80 Strand, London WC2R 0RL, England

If you purchased this book without a cover, you should be aware that this book
is stolen property. It was reported as "unsold and destroyed" to the publisher,
and neither the author nor the publisher has received any payment for this
"stripped book."

The scanning, uploading, and distribution of this book via the Internet or
via any other means without the permission of the publisher is illegal and
punishable by law. Please purchase only authorized electronic editions, and do
not participate in or encourage electronic piracy of copyrighted materials.
Your support of the author's rights is appreciated.

Text copyright © 2008 by Nancy Krulik. Illustrations copyright © 2008
by John and Wendy. All rights reserved. Published by Grosset & Dunlap, a
division of Penguin Young Readers Group, 345 Hudson Street, New York, New
York 10014. GROSSET & DUNLAP is a trademark of Penguin Group (USA) Inc.
Printed in the U.S.A.

Library of Congress Control Number: 2007034406

ISBN 978-0-448-44675-2   10 9 8 7 6 5 4 3 2

Chapter 1

"Ruff! Ruff!"

Katie Carew watched as her chocolate-and-white cocker spaniel, Pepper, jumped up and down near the tree in her backyard. He was barking at a gray squirrel on a branch above.

"Ruff! Ruff!" Pepper barked louder.

The squirrel opened its mouth and let an acorn drop. *Clunk*. It hit Pepper right on the head.

"Aroooo!" Pepper howled. He jumped up again.

Clunk. Down came another acorn. This one hit Pepper on the rear end.

That did it! "ARROOOOOO! RUFFFF! ARF!"

Pepper was barking *really* loud now!

"He wants to get that squirrel," Katie's friend Emma Weber said as the two girls watched Pepper leaping up and down on his hind legs.

Katie nodded. "But he won't catch him. He never does. It's just this game they play."

"He looks like he's having fun, though," Emma said.

Katie grinned. Pepper definitely seemed happy. His stubby little tail was wagging back and forth so fast, it looked like a brown blur.

"Arooo! Arf!" Pepper barked at the squirrel. He leaped up and down against the tree trunk.

"It's just that he's hard to draw when he's jumping," Emma told Katie. "He's not a very cooperative model."

"I know. All I've been able to draw is his ear," Katie agreed, looking down at her drawing pad. "The only time Pepper sits still is when he's asleep."

"Your dog is a lot like my twin brothers," Emma said.

Katie knew what she meant. Emma's twin brothers, Tyler and Timmy, were only a year old. They had just learned to walk. Now they never seemed to want to sit still. They were always getting into messes. Just like Pepper.

"Hey, look!" Emma exclaimed, pointing to the tree branch. "Now there are *three* squirrels up there. And they're all throwing acorns at Pepper."

"Three against one. That's not fair!" Katie shouted up at the squirrels.

The squirrels ignored her completely.

"Come on, Emma!" Katie said, dropping her paper and crayons and running over to the tree.

"What are we doing?" Emma asked.

"We're going to be on Pepper's team," Katie told her. She dropped down on all fours and started barking like a dog. "Ruff! Ruff!"

Emma grinned. She got down on all fours, too. "Arrooooo!" she howled.

"Arf! Arf!" Pepper barked.

"Ruff!" Katie barked. Then she wiggled her

rear end. "Look, I'm wagging my tail," she told Emma.

Emma dropped down onto her belly. Then she flipped over onto her back.

"What are you doing?" Katie asked her.

"I'm rolling over," Emma told her.

Katie laughed and rolled over in the grass, too.

"Animals have all the fun," Emma said.

"They really do," Katie agreed. "Nobody ever yells at them for getting dirty."

Emma wriggled out of her sweater, which had leaves and mud stuck on it. "Now I'm a snake. Get it?"

"Yes! Just like Slinky." Their class was learning about reptiles. Snakes like their class pet, Slinky, shed their old skin. Then there was a clean new skin underneath.

Katie got down on her belly and began slithering around in the grass. "Look at me! I'm a snake, too!" she told Emma.

Clunk. Just then another acorn fell from

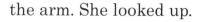

the tree. This one hit Katie on
the arm. She looked up.

The three squirrels were
sitting up there. They
almost seemed as if they
were laughing at her.

"That's it!" Katie
exclaimed, leaping back up onto
all fours. "Come on, Emma. Let's be dogs again.
Pepper needs all the help he can get!"

"Arff!" Emma barked.

"Aroo!" Katie howled.

"Grrrr ruff! Ruff!" Pepper growled.

That was enough to scare the three
squirrels out of the tree. They leaped
onto a nearby fence, and ran out of
the yard.

"Victory!" Emma shouted.

"Arooooo!" Pepper howled happily.

"Yes, Pepper. You're right. Dogs rule!" Katie cheered.

Chapter 2

"This is the best vegetarian chili I've ever eaten," Emma W. told Katie's mom later that evening. She stopped for a second and thought. "It's also the *only* vegetarian chili I've ever eaten."

"Vegetarian lasagna is yummy, too," Katie told Emma. "Oh, and veggie burgers. I love when Daddy makes those on the grill."

"Don't forget the grilled vegetables I pile on top of them," Mr. Carew proudly reminded Katie.

"Is it hard being a vegetarian?" Emma asked Katie.

Katie shook her head. "No. It's easy. I've

been a vegetarian for a long time."

"How come?" Emma asked her.

"I just don't want to eat anything that ever had a face," Katie explained. "I guess I stopped eating meat right around the time we adopted Pepper from the animal shelter."

At the sound of his name, Pepper came running over. He plopped himself down beside Katie and looked up, hopefully.

"I think Pepper wishes he had some of this people food," Emma said.

Katie gulped. "He does not!" she insisted. "He doesn't wish that at all!"

Everyone at the table stopped eating and stared at her. Katie turned beet red. She knew they all thought she was acting weird.

But it was just that Katie hated wishes.

It all started back in third grade on one terrible, horrible day. Katie had missed the football and lost the game for her team. Then she'd fallen in a big mud puddle and ruined her favorite pair of jeans. Even worse, she'd let out a huge burp in front of the whole class. How embarrassing!

That night, Katie had wished she could be anyone but herself. There must have been a shooting star overhead or something, because the next day the magic wind came.

The magic wind was a super-strong, tornado-like wind that blew only around Katie. It was so powerful that every time it came, it turned Katie into someone else.

The first time the magic wind came it turned Katie into Speedy, the class 3A hamster. After escaping from the cage, she wound up inside George's stinky sneaker. YUCK! Luckily, the magic wind had returned to switcheroo Katie back into a kid again, before anyone realized that she'd been running around the school— with nothing on but hamster fur!

The magic wind followed Katie everywhere she went—even all the way to Europe. When Katie was in England on vacation, the wind turned her into a guard at Buckingham Palace.

Those guards are trained not to smile no matter what the people around them are doing. But Katie wasn't trained for anything. And she didn't just smile. She burst out laughing—and got the poor guard she'd turned into fired!

Then there was the time the magic wind turned Katie into Pepper. She'd accidentally

broken a statue in her next-door neighbor's yard.

After that Pepper had to be on a leash if he wanted to walk anywhere! That wasn't very fair, since it was actually Katie who had caused the mess. Of course, Katie was the only one who knew that, so no one suggested she be put on a leash to go for a walk!

That was the biggest problem with the magic wind. It always blew in trouble. Then it was up to Katie to make things right again.

The magic wind was the reason Katie never made wishes anymore. But of course she couldn't explain that to Emma W. and her parents. They wouldn't believe her, anyway. Katie wouldn't have believed it herself if it didn't keep happening to her.

Still, she knew she had to say something, and *fast*.

"Um . . . I just mean Pepper is better off with *his* food," Katie told them. "This chili would be too spicy for him."

"That's true," Katie's dad said. "Dog food is the best thing for dogs."

"But people eat different foods every day," Emma W. insisted, "and all he gets is the same old doggie kibble in his bowl."

"Oh, I can fix that," Katie told her. She got up from the table and walked over to the cabinet where the dog food was kept. She pulled out a green bone-shaped doggie cookie.

"Pepper, treat!" she called out.

Pepper knew what that meant. He raced over to Katie, his little tail wagging.

"Sit," Katie said.

Pepper sat.

"Give paw," Katie said.

Pepper lifted up his right front paw.

Katie shook his furry hand. "Good boy," she praised her dog. Then she gave him the cookie.

Pepper swallowed it up in one gulp. Then he let out a little bark.

"You're welcome," Katie said with a giggle.

"How did you know he said 'thank you'?"

Emma asked her.

Katie smiled. "Oh, I just *think* I know what it's like to be a dog. Isn't that right, Pepper?"

"Aarf!" Pepper agreed.

Chapter 3

"Katie Kazoo, you gotta hear about this!" George Brennan shouted the next morning as Katie arrived at the school playground.

Katie grinned when she heard George using the way-cool nickname he'd given her last year. She loved the way it sounded.

"What's up?" Katie asked him.

"I'm gonna be a rock star!" George told her. "And so are Jeremy and Kevin. We're starting a band. I'm going to be the keyboard player."

"But you don't play the keyboards," Katie reminded him. "You play the tuba in beginning band."

George shook his head. "Not anymore. There aren't tubas in rock bands. So I'm switching. Kevin's switching, too, from trumpet to guitar. Mr. Starkey said it would be okay."

Katie nodded. Mr. Starkey was the band teacher. If he said it was okay, it must be. "But Jeremy's still playing drums, right?" Katie asked him.

George nodded. "You need drums if you're going to have a really rocking band."

Just then, Kevin Camilleri and Jeremy Fox—the other two boys in the band—walked over. Jeremy made two fists and began to drum in the air. Kevin played air guitar.

"Rock on, dudes!" Kevin exclaimed.

"Rock on!" Jeremy and George shouted back. Then they all went back to playing their imaginary instruments.

"What are you guys doing?" Suzanne Lock asked as she walked over to the group.

"Did you hear the news?" Katie asked her.

Suzanne scrunched up her mouth and

squinted slightly.
"What news?" she
asked kind of angrily.

Katie knew why
Suzanne was upset.
She hated it when
anyone found things out before she did. And
this time Katie was the one with the info.

"These guys have started a band!" Katie
exclaimed.

Suzanne looked over at the boys. George was still moving his fingers back and forth across his imaginary keyboard. Jeremy was drumming on nothing, and Kevin was rocking out on air guitar.

"They sound great," she joked.

"No, seriously," Katie said. "George is going to play keyboards, Jeremy is going to play drums, and Kevin is going to play guitar." She looked at the expression on Suzanne's face. "*Real* ones," Katie insisted.

"But they don't know how to play those instruments," Suzanne said.

"We're going to start taking lessons," Kevin told her.

"A fourth-grade rock band," Katie said. "It's going to be so cool."

"Do you want to join?" Jeremy asked her. "Maybe you could play bass guitar or something."

Katie smiled. Jeremy was a really great friend. He always tried to include her. But this time, Katie wasn't interested. "I think I'll stick with the clarinet," she told him. "I'm getting pretty good."

"Yeah, I heard you at beginning band practice," Jeremy agreed. "You sounded great on 'This Old Man.'"

"We're not going to play any of those old songs," George told her. "We're doing new, *rocking* songs."

"Our first single is going to be 'Lizard Rock,'" Kevin said. "We wrote the beginning of it on the phone last night."

"Lizard on a rock, listening to rock. Rock on!" the boys all sang at once. "That reptile's gone wild. Rock on!"

"That was deep," Suzanne said sarcastically.

"*I* liked it!" Katie exclaimed.

"Thanks," Jeremy told Katie. "We got the idea for it from studying reptiles."

"I figured," Katie said. "It's awesome. You guys can count on me to be your biggest fan.

And I want you to give me your autographs right now. Who knows? Someday you might be famous!"

Chapter 4

Katie walked into class 4A and sat right down in her beanbag chair. All of the kids in class 4A sat in beanbags. Katie's teacher, Mr. Guthrie, thought kids learned better when they were comfortable.

For Katie, the best part of having a beanbag chair was that the kids got to decorate them every time they had a new learning adventure. (That's what Mr. G. called lessons.)

Right now they were studying reptiles. So Katie had decorated her beanbag to look like a gecko—with a long green crepe-paper tail, brown and green construction-paper scales, and feet made of green felt.

Emma W. had decorated hers to look like a tortoise.

Emma Stavros had made hers look like a brown-and-white desert iguana.

Mandy Banks had turned hers into an amazing Komodo dragon lizard.

Kadeem Carter's was a rainbow-colored chameleon.

George and Kevin were sitting in matching crocodile beanbags.

And Andrew Epstein had created an alligator, which looked a lot like George and Kevin's crocodiles, but with a wider snout.

No doubt about it. Class 4A was Reptile World. But that was nothing new. All year long, Class 4A had been Slinky the snake's home.

As far as Katie was concerned, Slinky was the coolest pet in the whole school. Lots of classes had guinea pigs, hamsters, and gerbils in their rooms. But 4A was the only class with their very own snake.

"Okay, dudes," Mr. G. said, once all the kids

were seated. "Time for that awesome creative-writing assignment I promised you yesterday."

Katie sat up tall in her lizard beanbag. She loved any kind of assignment that was creative. Especially the ones Mr. G. came up with.

"I want you each to write a poem," Mr. G. continued. "And not just any poem. I want you to write a poem about reptiles."

Katie frowned. That was a tough one. Usually, she liked to write poems with words that rhymed. But what rhymed with *lizard? Gizzard? Schnizzard?*

And what about *gecko? Let go?* Not exactly.

Tortoise? Well that sort of rhymed with *porpoise.* Except not really. And porpoises weren't reptiles, anyway.

Katie's eyes drifted over to where Slinky the snake was lying in his cage. That was it! Katie would write a poem about the class snake. Lots of things rhymed with snake! She opened her notebook to a clean page and began to write.

SLINKY THE SNAKE

By Katie Carew

We saw an eggshell break,

And out came Slinky the snake.

So you could say maybe

He's our little baby.

He crawls on his belly

He's not slimy or smelly.

His skin has scales

To grip trees and rails.

Scales keep water out, too,

Like our raincoats do.

He's the best pet in school

I think snakes rule!

When she was finished, Katie read her poem from top to bottom. It was almost perfect. Except for one thing. Katie wanted to draw a picture of Slinky to go with the poem.

Katie looked over at the snake. He was lying quietly in his cage.

He'll be a lot easier to draw than Pepper, she thought happily.

But before Katie could pull out her colored pencils, Mr. G. clapped his hands. "Okay, dudes!" he exclaimed. "Finish up. We're going outside."

"Cool!" Kevin exclaimed.

"What are we going to do out there?" George asked.

"That's for me to know and you to find out," Mr. G. told him. "So line up!"

Katie closed her writer's notebook. What in the world could Mr. G.'s latest surprise be?

Chapter 5

"Okay, gang, here's the deal. We're going worm hunting," Mr. G. told the kids.

"What?" several kids shouted.

"You heard me. I want you to catch worms."

"What for?" Kadeem Carter asked.

"You'll find out in just a little while," Mr. G. told him.

"You mean we have to touch them?" Emma S. asked. She frowned. "That's gross!"

"Ooey, gooey, and gross!" George shouted out. But he sounded really happy about it.

Katie laughed. That was George. He loved anything that was disgusting. The more yucky, the better!

"But it's so muddy," Emma S. said.

Katie looked down at the ground. It *was* all wet and muddy. Having kids get mud all over their clothes wasn't something teachers usually did. Of course, Mr. G. wasn't a normal teacher.

The first week of school, Mr. G. made all the kids pretend to be birds and use their mouths as beaks to pick gummy worms out of bowls of chocolate-pudding mud. That had been lots of fun.

"The ground is muddy from the rain last night. You should be able to find lots of earthworms," Mr. G. continued as he handed out small plastic containers to each of the kids.

"What are these for?" Kadeem asked.

"When you find a worm, place it in your container," Mr. G. told him.

Katie took a container and went to work. She wasn't really grossed out by the idea of collecting worms. They were just like any other animals. And Katie loved all animals. Maybe her class was going to study worms in their next learning adventure.

"Oooo. There's a big fat one," Mandy told Katie. She pointed to the ground and made a face. "I can't touch it. Can you get it?"

Katie nodded. She picked up a twig and walked over to the slimy earthworm. She used the stick to push the slimy worm onto a dried leaf. Then she picked up the leaf and dropped the worm into her container.

"That was smart," Emma W. complimented Katie. "I'll try it that way."

Before long, each of the kids had at least one worm in their containers.

"I think I have the most," George said. "I've got three."

"I only have two," Kevin said. "But they're really big ones."

"Shouldn't we collect some leaves and dirt for the worms so they have something to eat when we bring them in the classroom?" Katie asked her teacher.

Mr. G. shook his head. "They're not going to

eat. They're going to be eaten."

Katie gasped. She wasn't sure she had heard her teacher right. "Eaten?" she repeated nervously. Her worms?

Mr. G. nodded. "These worms are a treat for our favorite reptile, Slinky."

"He'll like that," Kevin said happily. "I'm sure he's sick of the pieces of raw fish and crickets he usually gets."

Katie had never liked it that Slinky ate that stuff, but she'd never said anything. Still, this was different. She had found her poor, innocent worms. It would be her fault if they wound up inside Slinky.

"I don't want to feed my worms to Slinky," Katie said. "It's not right to feed one animal to another."

Mr. G. looked at her kindly. "I know how you feel, Katie. But snakes eat worms. That's how nature intended it."

Katie shook her head. "Slinky's not eating my worms," she said. "I wouldn't have collected them if I knew that was what we were doing."

"But . . ." Mr. G. began.

Katie was too upset to listen to her teacher. She poured the earthworms out of her container and watched them squirm back into the mud.

"FREE THE WORMS!" she shouted to her friends.

But the kids didn't hear Katie. They were already following Mr. G. back into the school— with their worms in hand.

Katie sighed. Those poor worms. They didn't realize they would soon be Slinky's lunch!

Chapter 6

"Oh yeah! We've got worms for lunch, too!" George cheered as he sat down at the table and looked at his lunch tray. He picked up his plate and jiggled it so his spaghetti moved around. "Just look at them wiggling around."

"Gross!" Suzanne said.

"Not as gross as what Mr. G. had us doing this morning," Emma S. said. "We were collecting muddy worms."

"That's disgusting," Suzanne said. She looked sympathetically at Emma S. "Too bad you're not in our class. We watched a movie about snakes."

"We get to watch a *real* snake," Kevin

argued. "Slinky. He's going to eat the worms after recess."

Suzanne looked at Katie. "Seriously?" she asked.

Katie sighed. "I don't want to talk about it," she said.

"Katie Kazoo refused to give her worms to Slinky," Emma W. explained to Suzanne. "She set them free."

"I can't kill animals," Katie explained. "Even if it's for Slinky."

"Slinky's gonna love *my* worms," George told the others. "They're really fat and juicy. Snakes have these cool jaws that open really wide. He's going to be able to swallow those fat old worms in one gulp!"

"George, you're making me sick!" Suzanne exclaimed.

George placed a strand of spaghetti in his mouth. "Slinky's gonna slurp the worms up, just like this!" The spaghetti wiggled and jiggled like a real worm as it moved toward his mouth.

"Cut it out, George," Katie said. She blinked a few times, trying not to cry. She felt so bad for the worms in the classroom.

She felt bad about disobeying Mr. G., too.

Basically, she felt bad about everything.

Just then, out of nowhere, Jeremy broke into song. "Lizard on a rock, listening to rock . . ."

"Rock on!" George and Kevin chimed in. "That reptile's goin' wild. Rock on!"

Katie smiled at Jeremy. She knew he had started singing just to change the subject. He wanted her to feel better. What a good friend!

"Hey, have you guys thought about a name for our band yet?" Jeremy asked George and Kevin. "I was thinking we could be called the Rhythm Rockers. After all, we're going to have a really good rhythm coming from my drums."

Kevin made a face.

"I think we should call ourselves George and the Jokers," George suggested.

"Why should *your* name be part of the *band's* name?" Jeremy asked.

"Because I came up with the idea for the band in the first place," George said.

"Yeah, but I'm the one who talked to Mr. Starkey," Kevin reminded him. "That's why he's letting us use the band room for practice. And I got him to promise to help us with our music, too."

Katie had once heard Mr. Starkey play the drums with his rock band, the Downhill Slide. He was a very talented musician. If Mr. Starkey was helping the guys, they might really become a great band one day.

If only they could stop arguing.

Katie really hated it when her friends fought. So she tried to tune out the argument and focus on her food. But after what George had said, the spaghetti just looked like a plate of tomato-covered worms.

This day was turning out so awful. The only good thing was that poem she'd written about Slinky.

The poem! Katie had almost forgotten that she'd wanted to draw a picture of Slinky to go with it. Maybe Mr. G. would let her do that during recess.

"Where are you going?" Suzanne asked as Katie got up from the table.

"Back to our classroom," she told her. "There's something I have to do."

"You'd rather spend recess in the classroom than out on the playground with us?" George asked her.

Katie nodded.

"Why?" Jeremy wondered.

"Slinky can't talk," she told them as she walked away. "Which means he can't argue, either."

Chapter 7

"Thanks for letting me stay here during recess, Mr. G.," Katie told her teacher a few minutes later.

"No problem," Mr. G. told her. "I think it's great that you want to draw Slinky."

"And I wasn't doodling in class like I used to," Katie reminded him. She wanted to make sure that Mr. G. knew that she usually tried to do what her teacher told her to. "I waited until recess to draw."

Mr. G. grinned. "I noticed," he told her. "Good job."

Katie sat down on the floor near Slinky's cage. She pulled a pencil from her backpack and began to sketch the snake.

It wasn't easy. Slinky's face was partially hidden by a big wooden tree branch in his cage. Katie wished he would wiggle somewhere else, so she could get a better view. But the snake was just lying there. And it didn't look like he was going anywhere anytime soon.

"I've got to make some copies of a story in the office," Mr. G. told Katie. "You can stay here and work."

"Okay," Katie told him.

"If you finish before I get back, just pack away your notebook and markers and go out to the playground," Mr. G. continued.

Katie nodded and went back to drawing. But after a few minutes, she stopped. Her drawing wasn't all that great. The problem was, she couldn't really see Slinky's face because it was blocked by the branch.

Katie tapped on the side of the glass cage, hoping Slinky would wake up and move. But it didn't work. The snake just lay there.

Katie sighed. If only she could take Slinky out of his cage to get a good look at him.

Deep down, Katie knew Mr. G. probably wouldn't want her to do that. But it would just be for a few minutes. She'd have Slinky back in his cage before Mr. G. returned from the copy machine.

Quickly, Katie removed the wire top from Slinky's cage. She reached in and gently lifted the small black, yellow, red, and white snake from the floor of his cage.

Slinky's body stiffened slightly at Katie's touch. She petted him gently as she placed him on her beanbag chair.

"It's okay," she told Slinky in a soothing voice. "I just want to draw you. I would never hurt you."

Just then, Katie felt a cool breeze on the back of her neck. She gulped. Cold air wouldn't be good for Slinky. He was a cold-blooded animal. His temperature changed to match the temperature around him. That was why there was a heater in his tank. Slinky had to be kept warm. A cool, breezy room was no place for a snake.

Katie would have to put Slinky back and figure out a different way to draw him up close. But before Katie could even pick up the snake, the gentle breeze grew stronger.

A lot stronger. In fact, it was a wild, whirling tornado!

A tornado that was spinning only around Katie!

Katie gulped. Oh no! This wasn't any ordinary wind. This was the magic wind. It was back!

The magic wind whirled faster and faster. It was so powerful that Katie thought she might be blown right out of the classroom.

Then, an even worse thought flashed in her mind. Slinky was so tiny and helpless. What if the wind blew him away, too? He'd never be able to find his way back.

But there was nothing Katie could do

about that. The magic wind wasn't something she could control. She shut her eyes tight and tried not to cry.

Then, suddenly, it stopped. Just like that. The magic wind was gone.

And so was Katie Kazoo.

She'd turned into someone else . . . one, two, switcheroo.

But who?

Chapter 8

Slowly, Katie turned her head. Oh no! The really cool red sneakers she had worn to school that morning were gone.

In fact, her *feet* were gone! So were her legs and her arms. Not to mention her hands, fingers, eyelids, and ears.

Katie couldn't hear a thing. But she could smell. And from where she was lying, she could sense the faint scent of food. She wasn't sure what kind of food, though. Katie stuck out her long, forked tongue to get a better whiff.

Her *tongue*? Katie gasped. How could she be smelling with her tongue?

Just then, Katie remembered something

Mr. G. had taught the class earlier in the week. There was one kind of reptile that smelled using sensors in its tongue . . . a snake!

That's when it hit her. The magic wind had switcherooed Katie into a snake. And not just any snake. *Slinky* the snake!

At the moment, Slinky was one hungry snake. His stomach was grumbling. Or at least Katie *thought* it was Slinky's stomach she felt grumbling. It was hard to tell where Slinky's stomach might be in his long, narrow snake body.

Wherever it was, it was empty. Now Katie wished she'd eaten some of that spaghetti at lunch. Too bad the food had reminded her of worms.

Although . . . come to think of it . . . right now a wriggly worm seemed tasty. Even though her Katie mind still thought it was wrong to eat animals, her snake senses were actually craving the worms. Kevin was right. Worms were definitely something Slinky would consider a treat.

But no matter how good those worms might taste right now, there was no way Katie could get to them. The worm containers were up on a high shelf. It would take a lot of wiggling for her to get up there.

Katie didn't have nearly enough strength to try that. She was so tired. She didn't feel like doing anything but sleeping. Yes! That sounded so nice. If she were home right now she would just crawl under the covers, shut her eyes, and take a nice nap.

But Katie wasn't home right now. So if she was going to fall asleep, it would have to be right here, in the middle of a cozy beanbag chair.

Aaaaahhhh. Katie opened her mouth wide and tried to yawn. Ooh. That felt awful. Like her skin was too tight or something. And she felt like she really needed to scratch.

If she were a fourth-grade girl again, she could have used a fingernail. But right now she didn't have fingers, never mind finger*nails*. If only she were still in her cage—well, *Slinky's* cage, actually—she'd be able to scratch her body on that wooden tree branch.

She looked around the room. The legs of the table that held Slinky's cage were wooden. Quickly she began wriggling her body, forcing herself to move toward the table.

The table seemed miles and miles away. But she was feeling more and more uncomfortable in her tight snakeskin. Katie just had to get to that wooden table leg.

So on she slithered.

And jiggled.

And turned.

And squirmed. Until, finally, she reached the table leg.

Yahoo! Katie thought to herself. I made it!

Katie placed her snake mouth against the wooden leg and moved her head up and down. *Scratch. Scratch. Scratch.*

Aaaahhh. Katie let out a hiss-like sigh. That felt much better. The itching around her mouth

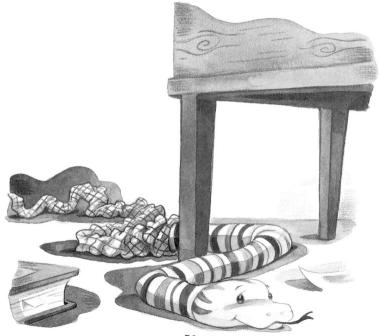

was practically gone now.

Unfortunately, the tight, itching feeling was moving down her body. Katie scrunched forward a little bit, so she could scratch lower down.

That's when she realized something. Her head felt different than the rest of her body. It was freer, and more comfortable. Like it was new skin.

New skin. She knew what that meant.

Slinky was shedding!

Which meant *Katie* was shedding.

Katie opened her mouth and hissed in fear. It wasn't as good as a cry, but it was all she could do right now.

Then she got back to business. Katie just had to get out of that tight snakeskin!

Scratch. Scratch. Scratch.

Chapter 9

Hooray!

With one last scratch of her tail against the wood, Slinky's old skin was completely cut open. Katie crawled out of it and slithered around joyfully. The new skin fit perfectly on her snake body.

Clomp. Clomp. Clomp. Clomp.

Just then, Katie felt strong vibrations coming from the hall. She couldn't hear the sounds, but somehow she knew what was happening. Those were footsteps. They were heading in her direction. Someone was on his way to Class 4A.

Oh no! It had to be Mr. G.! He was on his way back from the copy machine.

Clomp. Clomp.

He was getting really close now. Any second he'd be in the room.

When he got there, Mr. G. would see Katie's markers and her notebook on the floor. He would be upset that she had not cleaned up her mess.

But that was nothing compared to how angry Mr. G. would be to find Slinky on the floor instead of in his cage. When the magic wind came and changed Katie back into herself, she was definitely going to be in big trouble.

That is, *if* the magic wind ever came back. It seemed to Katie that the wind had left her in Slinky's body an awfully long time. Long enough for her to shed her skin completely, anyway.

What if this was the one time the magic wind decided to go away for good? Katie would have to spend the rest of her life shedding her skin and waiting for the kids in class 4A to feed her fish, crickets, and the occasional worm.

Hisss . . . Hisss . . . Katie let out the saddest snake sound ever heard.

Clomp. Clomp. Clomp. Clomp.

The vibrations in the hall were getting stronger and stronger. Which meant Mr. G. was getting closer and closer. Katie's little snake heart began to pound wildly.

Then . . . suddenly . . . the footsteps stopped. Just like that.

Phew! Mr. G. must have bumped into another teacher in the hall or something, Katie thought to herself. *They're probably out there right now talking about teacher stuff.*

At just that moment, Katie felt a cool breeze blowing on the back of her head. Almost instantly, her whole snake body grew cold— just like the breeze.

Katie began wiggling back over to the beanbag chair, hoping to curl up inside and warm up. But before she could squirm more than a few inches, the wind picked up speed, blowing harder and harder. In a second it became a powerful tornado that was blowing just around Katie.

The magic wind was back. And as scary as that wild wind felt, Katie was glad it had arrived. Once she was back in her own skin, she'd get Slinky back in his cage before Mr. G. returned to the classroom.

Katie braced her snake body against the magic wind. She didn't have to try not to cry— she knew she couldn't. There was nothing she could do but wait for the tornado to be over.

And in a few seconds, it was. The magic wind was gone.

And Katie Kazoo was back!

The first thing she did was wiggle all of her fingers and toes.

She sniffed the air—with her nose.

"Oh yeah!" Katie cheered. She shook her arms and legs and did a happy dance. It was so nice not to be a snake anymore.

Then Katie heard footsteps in the hallway. Mr. G.!

"Come on, Slinky," Katie said. "It's time to go home to your cage."

When Katie looked down at the ground, she didn't see Slinky. He was gone!

Quickly, Katie got down on her hands and knees and started looking around the corners of the room for Slinky. It was as if he'd just disappeared by magic.

Magic! Oh no! Had the magic wind blown him away?

It must have. There was no other explanation.

Which meant Slinky could be just about anywhere in the whole world. That magic wind was really strong.

Poor Slinky. He was in a new place, all by himself. He was probably really scared. And even hungrier.

Katie was scared, too. How was she ever going to explain this to Mr. G.—or to the other kids in her class? It was all her fault that Slinky had disappeared. They were going to be mad at her forever!

This was s-s-sooo not good!

Chapter 10

"Hi, Katie," Mr. G. said as he walked into the classroom. "Almost finished with your drawing?"

Katie frowned. She was finished, all right.

Mr. G. looked at her curiously. "What's wrong?"

"It's Slinky, he . . . uh . . ." Katie stammered nervously. "W–w–well, I was drawing him, but his face was hidden by that branch. I wanted to get a better look so I . . ."

"So you took him out of his cage," Mr. G. said, finishing her sentence. "Katie, you're not supposed to do that."

"I know," Katie said sadly. "I'm really sorry."

"We'll talk about it later," Mr. G. told her, sounding a little angry and disappointed. "Right now, I want you to put Slinky back in his cage." He looked around the room. "Where is he?"

Uh-oh! Now Mr. G. was going to be really mad!

"Th-that's just it," Katie stammered. "I don't know. I've been looking all over for him."

"What do you mean?" Mr. G. asked her.

"Well, after I took him out of his cage, he kind of slithered over to that table leg," Katie told her teacher. "He started rubbing his body on the wood. And then his skin popped open and he crawled out."

"Slinky was shedding right before your eyes," Mr. G. said. "That must have been very interesting to see."

"It was really tight and itchy," Katie said.

Oops. There was no way a fourth-grade girl could know something like that.

"I mean, um . . . er . . . he looked like he was very itchy. After that, I only turned away for a few seconds. Honest," Katie continued, tears welling in her eyes. "But when I looked down again, he was gone. Now he's probably far away, scared and all alone."

"Snakes aren't all that fast," Mr. G. assured her. "He's around here somewhere. A snake couldn't just disappear."

Yes, he could, Katie thought to herself. But

she really wanted to believe Mr. G. was right.

"There has to be a way to coax Slinky out of hiding," Mr. G. continued, thinking out loud. "We just have to figure out what it is."

Katie sighed. This wasn't going to be easy. After all, Slinky wasn't going to come running at the sound of his name like Pepper did. For one thing, Slinky couldn't hear. And for another, he didn't have any legs to run on.

Then, suddenly, Katie got one of her great ideas! "Slinky's very hungry," she told Mr. G.

Her teacher looked at her curiously.

"I mean, he must be," Katie corrected herself quickly. "We haven't fed him yet. And it takes a lot of energy to shed your skin. What with all that scratching and wriggling and all."

"True," Mr. G. said.

"I bet he'd come out for a worm," Katie suggested.

Mr. G. shot Katie a curious look. "I thought you didn't think we should feed the worms to Slinky," he said.

Katie nodded. "That's what I used to think. But now I understand that Slinky has to eat the kind of food that will keep him healthy. He's not like humans. We can choose from all sorts of foods and still stay healthy."

Mr. G. smiled. "Exactly."

"But I don't want to be the one to feed Slinky the worm," Katie admitted. "I just couldn't do that."

Mr. G. nodded understandingly. "I'll feed it to him. As soon as we find him," he added as he went up on the shelf and grabbed one of the containers of worms.

Mr. G. opened the lid of the container to let the scent of the worms into the air.

Katie imagined Slinky sticking out his long, forked tongue to get a good whiff.

Katie stood there beside her teacher, waiting for Slinky to slither out.

She waited.

And waited.

And waited.

But nothing happened.

"This is all my fault," Katie cried out. "Slinky is gone forever!"

Mr. G. shook his head and grinned. "Not exactly," he said. "Look over there."

Katie looked in the direction Mr. G. was pointing. At first she didn't see anything. But then she noticed something funny. Kadeem's backpack was lying open on the floor. And it was moving.

"He's in there!" Katie shouted out excitedly. "He's in the backpack!"

"Putting out the worms was a great suggestion, Katie," Mr. G. said. "He must have picked up their scent."

"With his tongue," Katie added.

"Exactly," Mr. G. agreed. He bent down and gently pulled Slinky from Kadeem's backpack. "Now let's get this guy back in his cage and feed him."

Katie turned her back when Mr. G. put a worm in Slinky's cage. She looked down at the floor and tried not to picture Slinky swallowing his prey.

A few minutes later, Katie watched as her teacher pinned Slinky's shed skin onto the bulletin board.

"Our little guy is growing up," Mr. G. joked. "He's gone up a size."

Katie giggled, picturing Slinky in a T-shirt and jeans—the kinds of things she and her mother went shopping for when Katie grew to a new size.

"Snakes are definitely lucky," Katie told her teacher.

"Why?" Mr. G. asked.

"They don't have to wait on line at a store to try things on," she answered with a laugh. "And their new skin is always a perfect fit."

Chapter 11

"Hey, Katie, where have you been?" Suzanne asked at the end of the school day. "I've been waiting outside the school for you for*ever*!"

Katie laughed. Actually, it had only been fifteen minutes since the bell had rung. As usual, Suzanne was exaggerating.

"I was cleaning Slinky's cage," she told Suzanne.

Suzanne made a face. "Why would you want to do that?"

"Because he deserves it," Katie replied. "He had a tough day."

"How tough can a snake's day be?" Suzanne asked her.

"Slinky shed his skin today," Katie explained. "You have no idea how exhausting that can be."

"And you do?" Suzanne chuckled.

Katie didn't answer. What could she say?

"Well, anyway, you missed everything," Suzanne went on.

"What's everything?" Katie asked.

Suzanne grinned. She really loved being the person who was in the know. "Well, for starters, the band broke up."

"Broke up?" Katie repeated. "But they just got together."

Suzanne shrugged. "And now they're apart."

"Was this all over that name thing?" Katie wondered.

Suzanne nodded. "Fourth-grade boys are such babies."

Katie sighed. "I sure wish I could help get the band back together."

"Well, you can't," Suzanne told her.

Katie looked at her strangely. Suzanne seemed almost happy about that.

"At least we still have the Bayside Boys," Suzanne said. "They'll always be our favorite group."

"I wonder how they got *their* name," Katie said.

"Oh, I know that. I read all about it on their website," Suzanne boasted. "They all grew up as boys in San Francisco. That's a city located on a bay. So they're the Bayside Boys."

"That makes sense," Katie said.

"It's a good name," Suzanne told her. "It really catches your attention."

Katie sure wished she could help the boys come up with a name like that. Maybe she could have helped them to keep their band together.

But Slinky had needed her, too.

Slinky!

Suddenly Katie had another one of her great ideas.

"Do you want to go to my house and look at the Bayside Boys website?" Suzanne asked Katie.

Katie shook her head. "I can't," she told her. "I have something really important to do at home."

"More important than the Bayside Boys?" Suzanne asked.

Katie nodded. "Believe it or not, yes," she said.

$\times$ $\times$ $\times$

When Katie arrived at school the next morning, there was a lot of tension on the playground. George was standing all by himself near the big tree glaring at Kevin. Jeremy was sitting on the bench, glaring at George. And Kevin was over by the swings glaring at Jeremy and George.

Katie walked over to Jeremy first. "I have a surprise for you guys," she told him.

"What guys?" Jeremy asked her.

"You and George and Kevin. The band," Katie said.

"There is no band," Jeremy told her. "We broke up."

"Oh yeah, Suzanne mentioned that," Katie admitted. "But I didn't believe her."

"Well, you should have," Jeremy said.

Katie didn't answer. Instead she took Jeremy by the hand and pulled him over to where George was standing. "Hi, George," she said.

"Hi, Katie," George replied. He ignored Jeremy.

"I have a surprise for the band," Katie said.

"There is no band," George and Jeremy said at once.

"Nice harmony," Katie told them. "That will come in handy when you're singing."

George and Jeremy scowled at each other. But Katie paid no attention.

"Kevin!" she called across the playground. "Come here."

Kevin didn't move. He obviously didn't want to be near George and Jeremy.

Katie took both Jeremy and George by the hands and pulled them across the blacktop.

"Stop it, Katie," Jeremy said.

"I don't want to talk to them," George insisted.

But Katie didn't stop until she reached where Kevin was standing.

"Hi, Katie," Kevin said, ignoring George and Jeremy.

"Hi," Katie replied. "I have a surprise for the three of you."

The boys all watched as Katie reached into her backpack. "Here it is," she told them as she pulled out three T-shirts. "Tada!"

"Wow!" Jeremy exclaimed.

"Those are so cool!" Kevin added.

"Amazing," George agreed.

Katie grinned. She knew the T-shirts were awesome. She'd spent all yesterday afternoon decorating them in red, white, yellow, and black. And she'd taken a really long time writing the new band name she'd come up with on the front.

"Slinky and the Worms," Jeremy read. "I like that."

"Yeah, it's funny," George agreed.

"No one will forget it," Kevin added.

"So now you guys can be a band again," Katie told the boys.

This time the boys didn't argue with her.

"We'll wear these at every gig we play," Jeremy promised her.

"Definitely," George and Kevin agreed.

Katie grinned. The band was back together.

"There's just one thing," Kevin pointed out.

"What?" George asked him.

"Which one of us is Slinky?" Kevin wondered. "I mean, I'd much rather be a snake than a worm."

"Yeah, well, so would I," Jeremy said.

"Slinky's not even your class pet," George told Jeremy. "You guys have a guinea pig."

"So what?" Jeremy asked. "I still think Slinky's cool."

"*I* think he's cooler," George told him.

Oh, no. It was starting all over again. Katie had to do something, and fast!

"Why don't you guys take turns being Slinky?" Katie suggested.

"Yeah, we could do that," Jeremy said.

"Sure," Kevin agreed.

George slipped on his T-shirt. "Katie Kazoo," he said. "You know what?"

"What?" Katie asked him.

"You rock!" George exclaimed.

Katie grinned. "Rock on, dudes," she said.

"Rock on!" Kevin, George, and Jeremy answered all at once. "Rock on!"

Surprising Snake Facts!

1. There are 2,267 known species of snakes in the world today.

2. Snakes are deaf, but they do feel vibrations in the ground they are resting on. (Surprise! That means a cobra can't really hear a snake charmer's flute. The snake moves because of the vibrations the music makes.)

3. Snakes can open their jaws so wide that they are able to swallow prey that is bigger than their heads.

4. The smallest snakes are Brahminy blind snakes. They only grow to about two inches long.
5. The largest snake, the anaconda, can grow as long as thirty-eight feet.

About the Author

NANCY KRULIK is the author of more than 150 books for children and young adults, including three *New York Times* bestsellers. She lives in New York City with her husband, composer Daniel Burwasser, their children, Amanda and Ian, and Pepper, a chocolate and white spaniel mix. When she's not busy writing the *Katie Kazoo, Switcheroo* series, Nancy loves swimming, reading, and going to the movies.

About the Illustrators

JOHN & WENDY'S art has been featured in other books for children, in magazines, on stationery, and on toys. When they are not drawing Katie and her friends, they like to paint, take photographs, travel, and play music in their rock 'n' roll band. They live and work in Brooklyn, New York.